I0630877

MAKE THE HOOD
GREAT AGAIN

By Rafa Wright

ISBN: 978-0-9960943-4-4

Published by Plug'd Media 2019

Detroit, Michigan

Content

The American inner city was created to separate the black from the white, rich from poor, the haves from the have-nots and never-wills. The acts done to us so long ago are still paying us extremely negative dividends today - mass incarceration, police brutality, poverty, poor physical and mental health, and disenfranchisement to name a few. It is a fact that people in the inner-city are the poorest, unhealthiest, ill-educated, overpoliced, wrongly jailed and imprisoned, and most hated against people in this nation. Until there are changes in this nation, this will continue. Fortunately, the change is possible because it comes from us.

No one can deny that our hoods are systematically designed to keep its occupants trapped and restricted from what the American dream promises everyone, which is equality, and the right to live a healthy, prosperous, purposeful life. The most damaging effect of living in the hood is how its designed to strip away your self-worth. This makes you hate yourself and the people around you. Where instead of you leading with love, you lead with hate. Without the use of statistics, we are all victims of this hate. We have all experienced the consequences. From a micro level, it hurts you every day. From a macro level, we lose our community.

All that said, the most known fact about life in America is that anything is possible. That "anything" can fall on the right or wrong side of the fence. Think about all the success stories of people making it out of the hood. Think about all the people who have beat the odds of living in the concrete jungle. Although the hood has always been a place where opportunity, resources, and outlets are as scarce as living in a third world country, there have been evidence proving that people of the hood's past were healthier, wealthier, happier, and more united versus today. Those many cases should be enough to motivate today's leaders in their efforts to make the hood great.

If nothing else grabs you in this introduction, I want the reader to think about this: How many times have we seen our dangerous hoods taken over by the same white elite who deemed our neighborhoods valueless in the first place? The same neighborhood where your father and older brother hustled, was put in prison or murdered, where your mother did drugs, where gangs had shootouts, where there were race riots, where you grew up on welfare, where you never had a chance to live a good life, will one day be on the national news as the next "best city in the world." Where redlining policies were created to take away all hope from the hood, revitalization policies are created to give hope to outside entities in our dangerous communities. Again, it takes away from the hood.

That dynamic alone should tell you something, that we live on valuable land. If an outsider can come into your hood and breath life in it, you can too. Will it be easy? No. Will it take time? Yes. Nonetheless, people from the hood possess the same ability to turn these neighborhoods into great places to live and prosper. The

Honorable Minister Louis Farrakhan always speak of how we can turn our hoods into paradise on earth. With all we know, the time is now.

Part 0: The Framework to Make the Hood Great

This section is this work's most subjective because all thoughts here are solely based on my thought and opinion. Although my thoughts are fueled from much study, research, and arguable evidences, everything is framed in opinion. Admittedly, this section dictates the direction of the remaining sections in this work. However, not agreeing with some or all of this section will not make this work's relevance to one null and void. In all, readers are asked to be as open-minded as possible while reading

this work, especially this section.

Common Myths about making the Hood great

Below are several myths about making the

hood great:

The hood doesn't need outside help

Any community can make itself great, the

hood included. With that said, the role of

outside entities, if utilized properly, can prove to be very advantageous to community development. Therefore, the thought that the hood only needs itself to become great is a fallacy. Although myth, outside involvement in community development is always a sensitive matter and should be executed cautiously.

Economic development is the only first step towards advancement

Historically, it's been the norm for communities to prioritize economic development as its first and most important steps towards community development. However, the hood should reconsider this, also including legal reform as an equally important priority. In fact, it has been recommended by many to work towards legal reform before economic development.

Although legal reform doesn't guarantee economic development, and economic development can occur without legal reform, most successful communities have strong economic foundations which benefited from policies which the community could benefit from. For the hood, there has been several disruptive policies which have been devastating to our communities.

Case: Redlining

Redlining was the federal government's successful effort to restrict African Americans to only living in poor ghettos across America. The modern-day hood was created because African Americans weren't allowed the ability to buy homes in suburban areas. Furthermore, redlining classed areas as favorable or dangerous, making places African Americans resided in as too risky to lend in. Although legal redlining was ended in the late 1960s, its damage is still felt today.

Case: Transportation

Policies around public transportation, and road conditions have been long disadvantageous to communities living in the hood. These policies have made it very difficult for inner city residents to find and keep work in suburban areas where there are higher clusters of jobs. Furthermore, governments have historically enforced more severe traffic penalties in poor inner-city communities versus more affluent communities. Lastly, auto insurance is usually higher in poor communities which affects how many can drive legally.

Case: Rockefeller Drug Laws, and similar statutes around recreational drugs

In 1973, New York Governor Nelson Rockefeller enacted harsh drug laws, particularly for small amounts of drugs in the state. Thought to be a successful measure to win the "War On Drugs," other states picked up these Draconian drug statutes. By intention, these policies disproportionately affected poor minority communities. As late as the Clinton administration, unfair drug laws were created. As a result, mass incarceration for poor black and brown people is one of America's biggest problems.

In all, in order to build communities in the hood, political and legal reform is required. It must be noted that reform is not to level a playing field where poor minorities and white Americans are equal, but instead is to grant our disadvantaged groups the access to needed resources and opportunities to build and maintain strong communities.

<u>Representation doesn't matter</u>

Some will argue that representation in community leadership don't matter. However, this is far from the truth. Solutions for the hood should come from people in and for the hood. This does not eliminate the assistance from non-represented parties, but instead reiterates the importance of representation in community development.

Hip-hop culture is detrimental to community development

There are many who are hypercritical of hip-hop culture, believing there are no positive aspects which will benefit inner city communities. Truth is, there are many positive aspects of hip-hop culture that's been proven to be pivotal to community development efforts in the hood.

Gangs shouldn't be included in the processes to make the hood great

Some believe street gangs and its members shouldn't be included in the processes to improve the hood. Truth is, many gang affiliates possess the heart, respect, and reach to be positive assets in making the hood great. In recent years, we've seen better social relations between traditionally rival gangs like the Crips and Bloods, and many others. Furthermore, there are several successful entrepreneurs, entertainers, educators, and activists who are or have been gang-affiliated. Instead of outright eliminating these entities from hood affairs, these positive leaders should be integrated into the causes to make the hood great.

The hood will never be great

This is perhaps the greatest fallacy spoke in the hood, that it can never be made great. Truth is, community development is very possible and today is the best time to act.

Cancers to all Communities

If nothing else, the one thing that has destroyed the hood is a lack of unity. Self-hate and envy have been bred in our communities for a long time. Even in past efforts to make the hood great, internal competition and in-fighting has destroyed all progresses made. When groups within communities hate one another, each group will constantly interrupt one another, even to the point of killing each other off.

Part 1: The Prerequisites

From the book *Community Building: What makes it work?*, all successful communities possessed these traits:

<u>Unity</u>

All successful communities are unified in love, and in passion to solve a problem.

Strong Leadership

All successful communities possess strong and effective leadership. Historically, the hood was able to look to religious and community action organizations for leadership. Today, these same leadership pools still exist, along with leaders from popular culture communities – rappers/entertainers, entrepreneurs, educators, and activists.

Awareness of Issues/Passion around Solutions

All successful communities are aware of problems in their community. Most of all, successful communities possess a mutual passion to solve the problems in their community.

Effective Communication

All successful communities are great at communicating with each other. Regarding communication, I am referring to residents effectively communicating its problems to leaders in the community, and leaders effectively communicating solutions to residents. In successful communities, communication is fast, transparent, and comprehendible to all parties.

Quick Assembly

All successful communities possess the ability to assemble quickly to plan and act.

Effective Training Practices

All successful communities have created training practices and processes to make sure everyone falls in formation quickly.

Able to adapt to new technologies

All successful communities are flexible and able to easily adapt to changing landscapes. Leaders can positively change with the times to sustain the community. Applying old, obsolete practices to problems will not solve them ever.

Therefore, successful leaderships and

communities possess the ability to

recognize new trends occurring to maintain

its success.

Operating within a small, concentrated geographic area

Communities are most effective when

operating within small geographic areas.

Therefore, organization within the

neighborhood or small areas is most ideal for effective community development.

History in Community Building

The strongest communities are usually following a precedent set by past generations. All successful communities have set morals, values, and systems. Communities with the greatest advantages are ones who can work off the foundation and successes of past leaders.

Part 2: The process to make the hood great

Step 1: The hood must unify

There should never be one n*gga that's the head of a crew because if that n*gga goes to jail, or gets killed, the whole crew goes down because everybody depends on one n*gga. But if everyone is equal and one person falls off, each member of the crew can give that member a little and it won't break anybody to put that member back on. You can't run nothing without no crew, and what crew is better than the n*ggas you grew up with?

-   Dame Dash

The first step towards making the hood great is unity. All community members are required to participate in improving conditions, no exceptions.

"There can be no black-white unity until there is first some black unity... We cannot think of uniting with others, until after we have first united among ourselves. We cannot think of being acceptable to others until we have first proven acceptable to ourselves."

– Malcolm X

What unity looks like?

Unity is realized when a community understands, loves, and celebrates its own people and culture. The hood must respect itself to make itself great. Once the hood is united this way, everyone will begin the action – assessing the issues and exploring possible solutions, together. **Truth: Most of the hood's problems stem from a lack of unity**. All struggling communities suffer from some sort of division. Therefore, the hood will be made great only when there is

unity among everyone in our communities.

Process: What sparks unity?

Unity happens in two ways: **(1) the hood**

simply unites, or (2) an event occurs that

forces unification. Most likely, because

division in the hood is longstanding and

deep, an event happening will be ideal for

unification.

EXAMPLE: Montgomery Bus Boycott of 1955

In efforts to end racial discrimination in America, the African American population in Montgomery, Alabama boycotted the city's public transportation system in response to the unjust arrest of Rosa Parks, a black woman who refused to give up her seat to a white man. The black population boycotted by avoiding city buses as much as possible, causing huge financial losses to the city's public transit system. The boycott lasted just over a year until local and Federal Governments desegregated the bus system.

Today, there's many issues that hoods can unify around, mainly political, economic, educational, and social disparities, racism, and acts of violence done against our communities. These are perfect reasons to unite and are more likely the issues that will ignite the hood's community.

Step 2: Organize (pt.1): Assembling Leadership

It must be stated that leadership does not equal superior in the grand scheme of improving the hood. Leaders in the hood are no better than the people they are leading. Leaders are servants to the community, not fame or financial gain. The ideal leadership for the hood is a leadership that's vigilant and uses their influence to improve everyone's life in the community.

Ideally, there should be a candidate pool of qualified leaders already existing in the hood. You know who they are because they are already visible and active. These leaders should have already been participating in some type of improvement efforts. Therefore, their knowledge of the mission – the problems and possible solutions should be fresh and relevant. These leaders are likely the best suited to complete the mission. Leaders who are not aware of the mission, the problems, and possible shouldn't be recommended.

All successful communities have effective leaders. **The most important traits needed in effective leadership are trust and experience**. These traits are manifested through the following competencies:

Representative of Community

All successful communities have leaders

from and for the communities they serve. A

represented, relatable, identifiable,

understanding leadership will be best

positioned to be effective.

Respected

Effective leaders are well respected.

Respected leaders can assemble

committed teams quickly, set rules and

norms easily without opposition, and are best positioned to prevent and/or diffuse issues internally or externally.

Diverse

Leadership should represent all walks of life in the community – age, gender, sexual orientation, religion, set, etc. If everyone is to benefit in a community, the leadership must embody all in the community.

<u>Vigilant</u>

All strong and effective leaders are committed to the well-being of the entire community. Successful leaders will always put the community's sustainability above personal accomplishment. Work done from successful leadership will reflect positive things happening to the whole, instead of the few.

Experienced Leadership

All effective leaders are experienced in leading groups, with experience in community development being a plus.

Ability to Collect Accurate Data

All effective leaders can collect the right data needed to solve a problem or problems. *What are the issues in the community? What are the possible solutions? Current technologies and processes used to solve specific issues?*

Can the community solve its own

problems? The most effective leaders have

systems and processes in place to

accurately collect real-time data to best

serve its community.

Effective Communicators

All effective leaders can communicate

issues, and solutions to their communities

in ways they can understand. Also, effective

leaders can use their communication skills to motivate and/or persuade followers to believe in specific causes.

Flexible and Adaptable

All strong and effective leaders can change with the times to stay successful.

Develop new leaders

Effective leaders will make sure new leaders emerge. Rather it's due to expansion or to fill a position after a

resignation or termination, effective
leadership will have processes in place to
develop and accept new leaders. In all, the
leader's role is to not only lead but to also
train his/her replacement to take the hood
to new heights.

Ability to kill beef within the hood

Leadership must be able to diffuse or
eliminate beef, whether it's internal or from
other parties within the community.

Leadership and their role in uniting rivaling groups

Knowing that organizations must form legitimately to make the hood great, its likely that many of these leaders are affiliated with traditionally rivaling groups – gang, religion, race, sexual orientation, gender, etc. In the effort to unite the hood, leaders from these other groups (sometimes rivaling groups), must work to unite everyone under one brand, one effort,

one mission.

The youth's role in making the hood great

Throughout history, efforts of social change always rode on the backs of the youth.

CASE: The Black Panther Party of 1966

African Americans had been victim to extreme police brutality for decades prior to 1966 which prompted Huey P. Newton, and Bobby Seale to create the Black Panther Party to monitor policing practices in black neighborhoods in their hometown of Oakland, California.

Making the hood great will be powered from the energy of younger generations

– millennials, and post-millennial generations, *also recognized as the hip hop generations.* Today's younger generations are equipped with more resources to build strong, sustainable communities than previous generations. Perhaps the greatest resource younger generations have is the internet. With the internet, all degrees of separation are either greatly diminished or eliminated altogether. With the internet, education has progressed exponentially, especially in economics/finance, social work, history, and the cultures. Lastly, the human capital is more plentiful than previous generations.

In all, the efforts to make the hood great will start with the youth. With energy, passion, fearlessness, the right resources, and the right guidance the youth will be some of the hood's greatest leaders on the frontline.

OG's role in making the hood great

While younger generations will naturally lead the efforts in making the hood great, it will be the older generations – generation Y, and pre-generation Y generations, with the experience, connections, and capital needed to be effective. Most of all, the hood's OGs are best able to enforce unity and order in the community.

These generations are to be mentors, councils, board members, protectors, and relationship catalysts for the hood. Of all the assets older generations possess, it's their respect that's most valuable.

The hood's OGs are to enforce geographic boundaries in our communities.

Furthermore, OGs should always work to yield peace and respect in the streets. As communities gain more control over the lands they occupy, these leaders must require parties to check in with their intentions in the community to keep efforts true and equitable. For outsiders, checking in consists of announcing one's presence and reasons for entering the community. For community members, checking in consists of submitting proposals of future goals to receive the hood's blessings.

Hip-hop's role in making the hood great

The role of hip-hop culture in making the hood great

There are two facts about hip hop culture:
(1) Hip hop culture is popular culture, and
(2) hip hop culture comes from the hood.
That said, there are many community
leaders in the hip hop world that can be key
in making the hood great. Many hip-hop
leaders possess the influence, connections,
and finances to push hood efforts ahead.
These leaders should be held high equally

to religious, political, legal, educational, or economic leaders in the community. If there was a leader who could form catalytic partnerships with all other leaders in the hood, it is the hip-hop leader.

These leaders should be using their platforms, resources, and finances to encourage hoods to unite and work together. Of monumental proportions, rival groups – mainly gangs (Crips, Bloods, etc.), religions (Christian, Muslim, etc.), education organizations, and business leaders uniting to make the hood great will always generate the widespread paradigm shift needed to elevate a community, and hip-hop leaders can be a catalyst.

Leadership by category

All hood leaders are to work for the community. It must be noted that some leaders may have a direct link to several core competencies – Political/economic, or political/education. For the sake of this work and the lists below, leaders are placed where their impacts will be most realized. The ideal leaders in the hood are:

Local politicians & legal officers

Leadership includes, but not limited to:

- **City managers** – mayor and/or city council.

- **Planning leaders** – economic development, housing, etc.

- **Public works leaders** – health department, water & sewerage.

- **Local law enforcement** – police, attorneys, and/or judges.

In totality, these officials play a role in how laws are created, adjusted, and enforced in our communities, as well as how resources are accumulated and allocated. Their understanding, compassion, and commitment to improving the hood will be key in their jobs being successful.

Economic leaders

The economic leaders in the hood are:

- **Entrepreneurs** – Creators of small businesses which creates jobs.

- **Investors & financiers** – Individuals who plant money into the hood.

- **Money managers** – Leaders who run financial institutions that can hold savings and lend money to the community.

- **Technical assistance providers** – professionals in accounting, startup, management, tech solutions, etc.

- **Consumers**

Economic leaders must work to bolster local small business, job creation, real estate development, and to ensure all consumer needs are met at the local level so that local dollars never leave the community. Consumers are to lead through their commitment to shopping local and supporting their own.

Education

Before outlining the ideal educational leaders for the hood, *education* must be defined. Broadly, the hood should ask, *"What is taught in the community?"* Specifically, education is manifested by *who is teaching, where is the teaching being taught, and what tools are being used to teach?*

Broadly speaking, everyone in and for the hood are educational leaders, from parents to children, manager to employee, neighbor to neighbor, etc. Specifically, the ideal education leaders in the hood are in the community's educational institutions – schools, training centers. These leaders are:

- **Teachers/Professors**
- **Counselors**

- **School Administrators**

<u>Social</u>

From a social perspective, all in the hood must exhibit leadership through morals, principles, integrity, passion, and love for self and others. Male leaders must show other men how to provide and protect in a masculine manner. Female leaders must show other women how to provide and protect in a feminine manner. Elders must guide the young. The young must protect the elders. Objectives of social leaders must be to:

- **Create healthier, wealthier families**
- **Produce more village-minded neighborhoods where neighbors take care of each other.**
- **Create more producers and conscious consumers.**

Specifically, ideal social leaders for the hood are more likely to come from:

- **Religious organizations** – Christian and Muslim religious leaders have been longstanding leaders in the community. The ideal religious leader is one who works from the pulpit and in the streets simultaneously. Religious leaders do not extract from its community. They invest in it.

- **Action organizations** – The hood's activists are fighting for civil rights for the people in the hood. Civil rights include fair treatment, and access to resources to maintain and grow the community.

- **Hip-hop culture** – Because people from the hood are often silenced, our inventiveness has forced us to use our art and creativity to speak about social issues. Therefore, the hood's creatives are social leaders that can use art as a display of social leadership. Art includes music, murals, film, poetry, interactive media, games, etc.

In conclusion to this social leadership section, one must reinforce the importance of vigilant leaders working as servants to the entire community. It is impossible to believe that corruption will never occur during this process of making the hood great because we are human. However, **what hedges leadership corruption is a strong moral and ethical code in the community**. What morals and principles flow in a community dictate what types of leadership it will breed. Traditionally in the hood, leadership has been more ineffective because there isn't a strong enough moral and ethical code in the hood. Not only is a strong leadership required to make the hood great, a code which embraces love and collective responsibility will also be required to take America's inner cities to new heights.

Step 3: Assess the hood's problems

Assessing problems in the hood

Once the hood has united, the next step will be to assess all the issues in the community. *What are the issues plaguing our communities? What problems require more urgency than others?* The hood will need to understand what's holding it back in order to make itself great.

Communicating what the issues are

Answering the questions, ***"What are the issues plaguing our communities, and what problems require more urgency than others?"*** will require the hood voicing what the issues are which can be easy or difficult depending on how effective communication is in the community. Effective communication channels for the hood are in digital platforms – internet, social media, etc., and physical platforms –

neighborhood meetings, city halls, rallies, school conferences, etc.

Common problems in every hood

Although different hoods are affected by different urgent problems, it is most likely hoods in America are suffering from the same problems which are causing the same consequences. These problems are:

- **Unjust political/legal systems** – unfair/extreme policing, systematic discrimination, and corruption breed consequences like, but not limited to police brutality, mass incarceration, redlining (poverty), ineffective healthcare, mental health trauma, and other issues.
- **Education** – What is being taught, who teaches, and what tools are being used to teach is a problem in

the hood. Inadequate educational systems in the hood breeds higher high school dropout rates and lower college graduation rates.

- **Economics** – Hoods in America have experienced mass poverty, mass unemployment, gentrification, economic extraction, a lack of local land ownership, and limited access to economic resources and opportunity for entrepreneurs and workers.

- **Social** – Along with a lack of unity, communities in the hood suffer from social disparities resulting from the above problems. Consequences of social unrest are poor health, high rates of crime and violence, uneducated populations, poverty, etc.

Advantages affluent communities have over the hood

Affluent communities have adequate access to resources necessary to maintaining a thriving community – **money, attention, technical assistance, and longstanding effective leadership**. A lack of resources, in the case of the hoods in America, can be attributed to systematic oppression. Most of all, privilege is the one advantage present in affluent communities that's not present in the hood. Nonetheless, making the hood great can be done without such privilege seen in affluent communities.

CASE: Tulsa, Oklahoma

Starting in the early 1900s, African Americans began migrating to Tulsa, Oklahoma and started to build their own community. During the oil boom of the 1910s, the entire state of Oklahoma flourished, especially the African American neighborhood of Greenwood in Tulsa, Oklahoma called "Black Wall Street." This community was home to many prominent black entrepreneurs, doctors, and

lawyers. In fact, the Greenwood community was

arguably wealthier than many white communities in

the state. At the height of Black Wall Street, there

were many thriving businesses, such as bus

services, restaurants, grocery stores, banks, and

law offices.

Lack of Respect

Most of all, there's a lack of respect

regarding the concept of the hood from the

inside and out. Historically, there has been

a lack of unity which has contributed to internal beefs, crime, and violence. Externally, outside parties have taken advantage of our lack of unity and resources which has lead to economic extraction, and the continual encouragement of us being divided. Reinstalling doctrines of respect will solve many of the problems mentioned in this section.

Step 4: Explore solutions, set goals, and establish missions

Establish Missions

Next, the hood must determine what are its missions are which should address the question, *what are the hood's problems?* Missions should reflect urgent, large issues. Because most hoods share the same problems, most missions will center around **health, wealth, education, and/or civil rights**.

Data Collection

After the hood has established its

leadership and missions to make the hood

great, the next step is to collect data from

the community – *What are specific*

problems within the bigger mission?

Specific statistics? Possible solutions?

What resources are being used to create

solutions? Are these resources currently

available in the hood or will leaders need to

search outside the community? How quick

can the mission be accomplished? Once data is collected, leaders can create action plans to make the hood great.

Action Plans

Action plans are small objectives within the bigger picture of making the hood great. Action plans should accomplish the following – *assembling and organizing resources, establishing teams, start and stop times of proposed plans, meetings, and benchmarks*. More experienced leadership will more likely have more effective action plans and execution success than less experienced leadership. That said, passion is equally weighted in successful action planning which can be argued to be seen more in less experienced, or more youthful leadership. Therefore, if experience and passion are the main determinants in a successful action plan, leaderships must strive to fulfill the right mix of managers – experience and passion to maximize action planning.

Propose action plans to the hood & execution

Once action plans are drafted, they must be presented to the hood for approval. This plan should be thorough. Everyone (leadership and residents) should use this time as an opportunity to ask questions, give feedback, and communicate as much as possible. If the hood likes the action plan, then the plan should be executed. If the hood disapproves, leadership should be given a fair opportunity to revise the plan. Once plans are revised and approved, execution should begin.

Step 5: Organize (pt.2):
Formally Organize

Formally Organize

Not referring to gangs which is the only organization most hoods see, there must be formal organizations created like small businesses, and non-profit organizations to execute the missions of the community. These formal organizations can receive the types of assistances that informal organizations can't – grants, technical assistance, etc.

<u>The ideal organizations that will make the hood great</u>

Broadly, the hood needs businesses and action-based organizations (for-profit and non-profit) to address issues directly like poverty, health, education, etc. Specifically, the ideal organizations to make the hood great are:

- **Community-development Corporations (CDCs) & Community-development Financial Institutions (CDFIs)** – Entities within a community that specializes in supporting local economic development projects. Funding, investments, and support are usually character-based which is most favorable to most aspiring economic change agents from the hood.

- **Business cooperatives & unions** – strategic partnerships and alliances designed to strengthen competitiveness among businesses in the community, and to ensure local businesses control as much local market share as possible.

- **Special interest/lobbying groups** – Advocacy groups dedicated towards addressing issues that affect the community exclusively. Applicable special interests in all hoods are political/legal reform, education reform, economic development, and human services.

- **Financial institutions** – Traditional financial institutions that's vested in community development.

- **Technical assistance providers** – Consultants in special skilled trades including but not limited to – accounting, management, community development, non-profit management, grant-writing, business compliance, etc.

- **Small businesses** – Formal businesses should be created to address community needs like but not limited to grocery stores, private medical practices (primary care, dental, mental), production plants, and leisure/personal pleasure businesses (bars, clothing stores, salons, barbershops, etc.).

- **Human Services Groups** – Organizations dedicated to physical and mental health.

- **Legal Clubs** – Legal clubs should be established to provided affordable legal services to the community. Legal clubs should include attorneys and paralegals to help hedge unjust legal processes to people in the hood.

- **Money Clubs** – Seen more in immigrant communities in America, money clubs/pools are crowd-investment vehicles designed as an informal financial institution to ensure economic opportunity is created in the community. These clubs circulate funds to community members to start businesses, buy homes, and/or care for their families. These loans are always laid back to the community, with interest. As a community grows,

so does the fund.

- **Other Neighborhood Organizations**

  – Other organizations in the hood

  should be dedicated to, but not limited

  to beautifying our communities,

  providing outlets for youth, self-

  policing our communities, and

  entertainment.

How should hood organizations connect with outside entities?

Organizations working in the hood should be strategic in how they work with outside entities. Ideally, the best working relationship between hood organizations and outside entities should be if hood organizations contract outside entities as consultants. In cases where hood organizations have developed projects that need additional resources, outside entities could provide that additional support. Hood organizations should not contract outside entities to save us or assist us without us pulling most of the weight. If the hood hasn't done most of the leg work on a project or initiative, it shouldn't contract with an outside entity under any circumstance. These outside entities' work must be representative of the communities that they will serve, with missions and objectives aligned with the missions and objectives set forth by the community.

Step 6: Execute Missions

Seeking help when needed from outside entities

The hood should only seek outside assistance in an emergency. What's important here is to make sure assistance is needed in the first place. Moreover, hoods must make sure they are really receiving assistance and not being taken advantage of. Respected communities with respected leaders are less likely to be taken advantage of when leveraging outside assistance versus less respected communities. In most cases, the best way to leverage help from outside entities is in the form of technical assistance.

Nationwide, most hood organizations are least effective in legal, especially as it pertains to real estate acquisition and development. Other skills to consider when seeking technical assistance is management (for-profit and non-profit), strategic planning, grant writing, and IT.

What's important here is ensuring that consultants performing technical assistances are the best qualified to perform the service, and that the skill that's being learned is best suited for the mission or goal at hand.

Establish teams

After hoods have set goals and objectives to be accomplished, leadership must establish teams to start working. These teams will tackle the many complex problems to achieve the goal. What's important here is making sure the teams established are the right teams for the mission, and that the right members are a part of the right teams.

Assess Resources

The next step is to assess all available resources to get a better handle on how to affectively allocate them. What's important here is properly aligning resources with the right missions and goals. Most importantly, organizations and groups must make sure they aren't competing for resources. To prevent this, organizations must find ways to consolidate efforts to better utilize resources used by multiple groups.

Strategic Planning

After teams are established, the next step is strategic planning. What's important here is ensuring all plans are tested and proven to the team's best ability before executing. Teams must perform the proper due diligences to reduce chances of error.

Fundraise

Organizations will need to raise funds to execute the missions at hand. Strong communities can fundraise internally without searching for funds from outside sources. What's important here is ensuring that funds are coming from the right sources, with the right terms, for the right purposes, in the right hands.

Strategy Execution

The last step is to execute the play set. What's important here is staying true to the agreed upon plan, no matter what. Most importantly, a key component of strategy execution is maintaining record of successes and failures during the entire execution process – *planning, team assembly, technical assistance, fundraising, and actual execution. What strategies should be continued? What strategies should be removed? What worked? What didn't work? Who was most effective within the working groups? Who was least effective?* Besides actually executing the plan, reflection on what worked and what didn't is perhaps the most important task in this process.

Conclusion

Broadly speaking, anyone interested in making the hood great, or any community for that matter can utilize this work. Whether one is a leader or not, everyone plays a role in building and maintaining a community. There are roles to be played in making the hood great, and this work aims to establish what those roles are, who should fulfill them, and what actions should be taken.

Specifically, there are some characters who should find interest in this work for motivational purposes if nothing more. Will this work answer all questions to the issues in community development for the hood? Most likely, no. But what this work will do is start to lay a foundation for current and future change agents in the hood. After reading this work, a conversation should be sparked in our communities on where we begin, with who, where, and how. The "why" is stained on every page. All that's left is us doing the work.

Lastly, if nothing else, this work should be used as a present example of current efforts and actions to improve conditions in America's inner cities. If what's presented in this work proves to be insufficient, this work can at least show someone was thinking and moving progressively to change life in the hood. If what's presented in this work proves to be effective, then this work should be celebrated, but also stored and refined so that its relevance will remain for future generations.

As I stated earlier, if there was ever a time to act on improving the conditions in our inner-city communities, it is today. With the masses rallying behind their own respective agendas, it is time for the people from and for the hood to rally behind elevating our communities for ourselves, our children, and all future generations.

www.ingramcontent.com/pod-product-compliance
Lightning Source LLC
Chambersburg PA
CBHW020916180626
46816CB00007BA/2432